The Embalmer

❧

by Anne-Renée Caillé
Translated by Rhonda Mullins

Coach House Books, Toronto

First English edition. Originally published in French by Héliotrope as
L'embaumeur by Anne-Renée Caillé.

Coach House Books acknowledges the financial support of the Government
of Canada through the National Translation Program for Book Publishing,
an initiative of the Roadmap for Canada's Official Languages 2013–2018:
Education, Immigration, Communities, for our translation activities. We are
also grateful for generous assistance for our publishing program from the
Canada Council for the Arts and the Ontario Arts Council. Coach House
Books also acknowledges the support of the Government of Canada through
the Canada Book Fund.

LIBRARY AND ARCHIVES CANADA CATALOGUING IN PUBLICATION

Caillé, Anne-Renée, 1983-
[Embaumeur. English]
    The embalmer / Anne-Renée Caillé ; translated by Rhonda Mullins.
Translation of: L'embaumeur.
ISBN 978-1-55245-378-0 (softcover)
    I. Mullins, Rhonda, 1966-, translator II. Title: Embaumeur.
English.
PS8605.A404E4213 2018   C843'.6   C2018-903963-9
                                    C2018-903964-7

The Embalmer is available as an ebook: ISBN 978 1 77056 577 7 (EPUB), ISBN
978 1 77056 578 4 (PDF)

Purchase of the print version of this book entitles you to a free digital copy.
To claim your ebook of this title, please email sales@chbooks.com with proof
of purchase. (Coach House Books reserves the right to terminate the free
digital download offer at any time.)

Yes, there are cases, the soldier, the brothers and sisters, the bodies of stones, the drowned, the suicide victims, the sick, the murdered, the killed. We will come to them, they will all come.

❧ 1958, a small town.

One person dies every month. That's the average.

Every month, there is a viewing at the funeral home. There were few, if any, cremations in those days, just viewings. It was a matter of belief.

He is seven years old at the time, he likes going to the funeral parlour to see the body on display, likes the viewing. He doesn't always know the body, but he likes to go, to see it, and, soon, to touch it.

Kneeling on the prie-dieu in front of the open casket, he looks at the corpse and then looks around the room, carefully, to be sure no one sees him when he touches the corpse with a finger.

He touches the corpse.

I remember the name of the first corpse I touched. He tells me his name.

❧ He tells me of the power of the attraction.

When I would see a hearse go by, I couldn't take my eyes off it until it turned the corner and was out of sight.

🍃 A car with seven or eight people in it.

The average of one death a month changes that day. A family, I think. Hit by a train.

In that moment, the average of one death a month grows, seven or eight at once, because they all die, they all die together.

That month, the attraction grows too – the trigger, he says.

The accident is the trigger.

꙳ Prompted by: a child wanting to keep company with the dead.

My father is that child, I will not keep repeating over and over, my father tells me, my father does, my father goes, says, did, says... He will be the child, the man, I will call *he*. He will blend in with the dead at times. We will recreate his connection with them. We will have to recreate it. We will do it as a matter of course.

❧ Behind the house, a rabbit hutch.

Empty. One morning he decides he needs space.

He decides after the train, the morning he decides is after the train. The rabbit hutch has been abandoned for a few years, his older brothers and sisters have left the house, empty. Animals are no longer bred.

Explains that the females and their young were kept in there for the first few months, far from the males who tend to kill their young so they can possess the female. The males are kept in a big cage.

The space is repurposed.

He sets up in the abandoned space.

Small table, small tools, frogs, and other dead things; a first lab, where male rabbits, female rabbits, young rabbits slept, ate, hopped.

Later, looking back on this child's play with dead animals, he tells me it didn't last long. You know I always loved animals, I never felt right hunting with my brothers. At some point, they didn't know, I stopped putting bullets in my rifle.

I just wanted to be in the woods.

❧ 1966, his first embalming.

Two, actually: the stars align, a family trip during which he finds himself in a funeral parlour in a big city. His older brother does their accounting.

He goes straight to the lab. He is invited in by the undertaker, he is fifteen, and he looks, he looks at everything he can, procedures, incisions, liquids going in and coming out.

From where he stands he can smell, he can see, he even helps dress the body, tells me of his fascination.

Back from his trip, he immediately sets off to the local funeral parlour. Not just to touch a corpse this time, this month's corpse. He will offer his help.

I had to work there no matter what.

I would go to school, I would make hay, and then I would drive the ambulance, the hearse, pick up the dead from their homes, bring them back, help with the embalming.

I didn't have my driver's licence.

❧ That was the beginning.

It's a beginning, the one I have chosen – anyway, it doesn't tell the whole story. I am not him. This is not an investigation. I am not studying him. I am looking at what can be seen. I am listening to what can be heard: a child who keeps company with the dead and an adult who keeps company with the dead, who chooses them. It was not even father to son. It was not even the family business, as is usually the case.

I would like to know what that means and whether that means anything at all.

≈ I will ask him whether he understood in hindsight.

Why he chose this work. He will say it remains a mystery.

With no segue he tells me about the psychic, about the old recording he has of their encounter, when she tells him that he didn't choose this work by chance, that it was to atone for sins he had committed in past lives.

Orgies of blood, she had said. She simply channelled the three voices; they knew me better than I know myself.

I lose the train of thought a little at this point, but I leave that alone. It has to be left alone.

What I call the beginning is a child who wants to get close to the end, the final moments, to piece back together something of the man, the woman, the child, of the one who is no more.

So what can he piece back together?

It requires faith in make-believe. But not for my father.

What do we truly believe, faced with the makeup, the Sunday-best clothes, the hued skin, the carefully chosen jewellery?

You have to be true, to be faithful to the photograph the family sometimes leaves. I am surprised to find out this is not done consistently.

But we will need to discuss the photo the loved ones may leave, a photo of the dead person alive, still there, a photo that testifies with its colours and its inspiration. It must be the best picture.

Because it will be the last time, the dead's, their last.

And the last chance for loved ones to be in their presence, although presence might not be the right word.

Discuss fidelity in reproducing the living, the actual colour under the eyes, white, grey, green, blue, and so on, which the dead soak up, take on, circumscribe, and the colour he has to give the dead, for this time, the last time.

What are the colours of advancing death, I have to ask. We will have to talk about colours again, he will tell me about them, and what he does with these encroaching colours that jostle with those of the photo.

ᕤ When it's over, you get a plastic bag.

With the ring, the tie, the lipstick, the scarf, the earrings: you leave a list of what you do not want to be sent underground, to the fire.

And the pictures displayed beside the open casket. The shock they create.

What you don't want to be buried or what you want to stay buried.

What is important to bury with her, with him.

Later I think back to that woman who asked him to put her husband's favourite dinner in his casket before it was lowered into the ground: a cheese sandwich, two beers.

I ask him again about the photo. Is it really like that? Yes, if you like, it helps. It has to be as natural as possible, but even without a picture, it's a matter of judgment, erasing the disease, the traces of death, fattening up the wasted. Sometimes there is a hollow of up to two inches at the temples. Makeup is only the surface, the finale. I would add the colour at the beginning. You have to watch the amount of tinted powder. It's red, it stains. It comes in a little packet, like ketchup, he says. You prepare the recipe, you inject the liquid, and the body and face take on the colour. The body reacts at different rates; it depends on the illness, the general health, because it flows through the bloodstream. The colour appears at the surface of the skin.

❧ I would see the family after the embalming. They would often ask him to explain what had been done, to discuss the results.

I remember an aunt who had had cancer. She was fairly young, but she had been sick a long time. She was unrecognizable. Even at the age of fifteen, I thought the embalming was botched, the viewing obscene. And my family was taking dozens of pictures to remember her by.

I would have demanded to see the embalmer.

❧ I feel like I take, I unload, you unload, I unload some more.

Perhaps we are just transferring weight back and forth. You will use the word *heavy* at one point.

⅋ He has a list of cases in hand.

We talk about it over breakfast at the diner, descriptions, conditions, facts. For the first time we talk about cases other than by pure recall.

He has given them a name, each one, a name.

Between these deaths, we don't know, I don't know, what will be said. Although there may be an inkling, but it's mine alone. This simulacrum may be the thread that unites the dead, our dead, who expect unveiling, a return, a telling. But when you come down to it, the dead expect nothing from us. The simulacrum isn't just the makeup. It isn't just death that slips insidiously inside a body. Nor the illusion that ensnares us. Nor the idol that remains and is substituted for others. It is also all that will not be said, all that will be kept quiet.

Is there an order to the cases, a structure? It is his order, the order of the dead as they make each other's acquaintance.

I tell myself that at least we won't put the suicide victims with the other suicide victims.

They are listed, he reviews them and chooses. It will not be a chronological selection but something like natural selection, that of a memory marked perhaps. I let him do it, let him navigate alone through the list.

❦ And I am still wondering what I should call him. By him, I mean my father.

Who cuts, applies makeup, opens, stitches, looks at pictures, tries to be true to the living, the dead, and the work. I don't know what goes through his mind when the flesh has disappeared, when a face is shattered, when they are bloated or burned, and you have to be true, make it true, when half of the body has exploded and there is virtually no skull left, and you have to get it right.

You have to show what the dead person was before the fatality, the tragedy, the destiny, the call – whatever name you care to give it. I string these words together and I don't think about it anymore. I think of nothing. No matter the names.

Or what he was before: before the train, the cancer, the fire, the gunshots, AIDS, the grenade, asphyxiation, the wave, the weariness, giving up.

Before: suffocating, getting caught in the trap, being paralyzed.

❧ There are precautions to take.

Of course, details have to be changed, public archives checked – maybe I will go that far, but no name, place, date.

But we protect ourselves, too. These stories aren't always tidy, there is what is unimaginatively, plainly called pain, violence, betrayal, lie, camouflage, bestiality, fear – these words are nothing, are a big hole in the story.

❧ Saint-Jean-de-Dieu.

A call. A body in a bedroom has to be picked up. A woman in bed with an expression on her face. Fear.

She died with her hands near her face, small hands, fingers and arms that won't unfold. It's fear. Her hands are frozen that way, her arms won't unfold.

He has to break them.

Normally, the arms, with their muscles, their nerves, their skin, their tissue, unfold, normally the joints unfold, but this time they don't. In fact maybe she died with arms that already wouldn't unfold. She is frozen in movement and her face, too, is clenched.

He has to break them. There has to be a viewing.

For the family, break the arms. Break the arms for the family. Break the arms for the goodbyes. It was, if you will, an order.

The arms weren't broken. The casket was closed. He told me.

◈ The village has a new priest.

Parish visits to houses along the country road, the annual blessing of children. But the next year he skips a house on the road, moves directly to the next house, a small skip, skips a house for years to come, my grandfather's. Who went to mass every Sunday, gave his twenty-five cents. He would give me five cents. I would make the coin jingle against the others in the basket. But I kept it in my palm.

But my grandfather never wanted to kneel before the priest to be blessed.

So sometimes a blessing is no longer deserved.

One morning, in another house along the road, a man is found dead, a neighbour, a father of seven. Blessed.

It is death by hunting rifle, a suicide. We knew, he knew, he told me, I knew the man's body was buried… Everyone knew, and that was clearly the desired effect. The body was buried in the parish cemetery and in the cow pasture.

'Thou shalt not kill.' Exodus 20:13.

The casket is two metres long. It's easy enough to calculate. One metre in the cemetery and the other, the rest, in the neighbouring field. Which part of the body is in the cemetery, which part is in the field, is not said.

❧ He was a man of the cloth.

And his head to be rebuilt. It comes in flattened, deformed. He tells me it really had to be rebuilt, truly in pieces, reconstructed, a jigsaw that would take eight hours. A real puzzle.

I started by removing the brain, drilling, piercing, stapling, rebuilding the inside of the skull with plaster. The stitches have to be inside, invisible, the plaster has to be sanded down.

Did he have to create the head from scratch, imagine its shape? The first clue to get the angle right is the scalp, and from there the head has to be invented.

The other bodies that arrived that day had to be entrusted to other hands. The head had to be ready for that very evening, the refashioned head had to be displayed that very evening, without fail.

There were always a lot of demands.

❧ A soldier is repatriated.

The body of a Canadian soldier who died in combat, the story goes that there was an accident, a helicopter explosion, the body is repatriated as is proper in a shipping casket, airtight, watertight, lead-lined.

After the military funeral, there's a request for the body to be cremated, but lead cannot be put in the cremator, so the body has to be transferred to another casket and then incinerated.

This would have been done, it would have been, if the casket hadn't been filled with rags and rocks.

I say I don't understand, and he tells me the body was not found and they didn't have time to look for it or it couldn't be put back together again.

The choice of rocks speaks volumes.

What I retain: make them believe in the body, in the weight of the body. What we should retain: a body that weighs the weight of the rocks, kneeling before the rock, returning to rock, that's it, that is always it. For a while I feel sorry for the duped loved ones, that is precisely it, being fooled in front of a closed or open or empty box. Because what really remains?

❧ He thinks and adds.

At times he had to display an empty casket: the body hadn't arrived in time, things didn't go as planned. In such cases they had to be sure to properly seal the box.

I am thinking of one time, a murder I think, the morgue hadn't released the body in time for the service, the casket was empty, but the family knew it.

Even more so than when faced with the embalmed, when faced with a closed lid we believe in a body of flesh, of air, or of rocks.

❧ I find viewings repulsive.

A viewing offers nothing, only takes away everything, takes away even more if that is possible, because from that point on what is left is nothing, a casing hollowed of its flesh.

I prefer a closed box.

I think of the rosaries my aunts would give me.

I never understood rosaries, statues, effigies of St. Jude that I was supposed to keep in my wallet, not because I don't believe, though I don't believe, but it is almost the same for the embalmed.

The one you love is no longer there.

The one you pray for is no longer there.

Why bother with an intermediary, what is in between?

I still have in my wallet the tiny reproduction of St. Jude. Two centimetres square. Yellowed.

In a hand-stitched plastic envelope.

∾ It is sensitive.

The story is sensitive, they all are, but some are more disturbing.

Cadets train to use grenades: the purposes, the uses, the damage caused by the blast.

Apparently a grenade, one that explodes and maims, destroys the enemy, blows them up, disfigures, burns. This is the story of an oversight.

An active grenade left in the box. Detonated in the face and body of a cadet and those around him, grenade in hand, the cadet was nothing but bone.

Dead teenagers. Dozens of wounded.

Meanwhile I read that it had been left among the practice grenades, that a cadet had pulled the pin as a joke. That is the one he chose.

I read that this type of training was normally done outside, but that it was raining that day. I also read that the building wasn't damaged because the cadets absorbed the blast. An afternoon that made the damage from a grenade tangible. Unforeseen viewing.

And the story of a long night at work and guards at the door to the lab to ensure he was the only one to go in there, because something had been forgotten, overlooked.

——— ———

Several survivors suffered trauma. It seems some killed themselves.

The amount allocated to the boys' families for funerals was calculated parsimoniously, not one cent more than necessary.

❧ It's a small world.

A man takes a seat in a hotel dining room, a hitman. A second man approaches and tells him to move to the bar without another word, that he is in the line of fire, there are going to be fireworks, we are going to clean house.

A few minutes later, two people are killed.

Between hitmen, a bond.

A small world. The first man tells him the story as if telling a completely different story, any old story, a mundane tale.

This detail remembered: he had an apartment for every day of the week. It seems excessive to me, but is it?

When he said it must take a lot of guts to be a hitman, the hitman answered no, but to do what you do, messing with bodies, that takes guts.

❧ A private home.

Sometimes he had to go get the body at home, at home under the sheets, with the family. It takes a lot in the end for the family to let go.

The body is in there.

They told him the man died eight hours earlier, or in fact the family said that to the doctor, who wrote it on the death certificate. The hearse left with the body, the work must be done quickly, the family wanted the viewing to take place that very night.

The first cut, the carotid. Then injecting the formaldehyde, which goes straight to the brain, the fingers, hands, joints of the arm start moving, there was still oxygen in the brain, I say excuse me, my friend, as I continue to inject the formaldehyde.

There is no way he died eight hours before, it must have been an hour at the most – when recovered, the body was still too warm, with that fever that comes on right near the end. It should have been a clue.

Of course he was dead. He hesitated for a moment

when he saw the hands move, he just wasn't quite ready for the big masquerade.

So he learned not to believe closed eyes, doctors, death certificates, family, because there are demands, desires to fulfill, and the family has no scruples about lying.

❦ Two children playing in an alley.

Brother and sister, it is not said, playing hide-and-seek, it is not said either, but we can easily and uneasily assume. Because people looked for them and couldn't find them.

In the end it took hours to find them.

In an old fridge, dead from asphyxiation.

An old fridge, one of the ones that can be opened only from the outside, the ones that latch when they close.

Twenty-five years later, this image during a bike ride: in an alley he sees one of those fridges with tape around it, several rounds of tape.

And I think of protective tape, tape that safeguards.

It is to avoid thinking about what might have happened inside the fridge that day: at first laughter, little faces and hands, and then wails, screams, terror.

One morning, I notice for the first time these words in my fridge, on the left, in red:

Your new appliance has a safety door that can open from the inside. PROTECT YOUR CHILDREN. *When disposing of or storing your old appliance (fridge, freezer, dryer), remove the door. Issued in the public interest.*

❦ A woman sets fire to her house.

She wanted to burn everything but she didn't want to burn, she wanted to die, she just wanted to get the fire started. Let the rest go up in smoke.

Goes into the basement, gun in hand, opens the freezer door, gets in, closes the door, and shoots herself in the head.

A house turned to ash with a suicide victim in the freezer.

❧ Organ donation.

It happens at the morgue. Harvesting, sending the organs to the banks. I think kidneys, liver, heart.

He tells me the body could arrive hollow. A particular hospital, he names it, helped itself to more than the others, knees and spines replaced with bits of wood.

I hear: there is no problem with organ donation. There is just uneasiness when faced with a body where everything has been taken. That's how he said it, taken.

Remembers: a body is laid on the table ready for embalming. He gets a call telling him to wait, not to touch anything.

They will come and take the eyes.

He stops. I ask what he did after that. About the holes left behind.

From that point on, it would happen fast.

There was leakage. Stopping the flow is important. Fill the orbit with cotton, for the shape and to prevent collapse. It will support the plastic eye cap, its little claws clinging, use a hypodermic needle to inject a liquid that thickens the skin. At the end make sure the eyelids are properly glued.

And the 'eyes' are sealed shut.

❦ A body is repatriated from Mexico.

A drug dealer, they say. He is still saturated in formaldehyde and was sliced open from top to bottom, from chin
to pubic bone, a single, long incision. An oddity, he
explains, when you are used to the Y cut of autopsies
around here.

He gets a call: according to the man's loved ones, he
should have had five thousand dollars on him. The
dealer was wearing jeans, no lining. He goes over the
body with a fine-toothed comb, nothing. The money
must have been collected down south. There was a single
long incision.

Autopsia: seeing with your own eyes.

There was nothing to see.

❖ A car accident.

A body catches fire, they ask him to dress it before it goes in the casket, which he refuses to do. There is no more body, the bones are blackened and brittle, he can't, the body will be placed as is in a closed casket.

At the funeral home, the family will force the casket, will put clothes on a charred corpse. The casket will be closed again.

&a; After the viewing.

A casket is placed in the hearse, driven to the church for the religious ceremony before burial.

It was a quiet Monday morning. Sometimes I would drive if no embalmings were scheduled. We would go to a restaurant during the ceremony.

I thought I saw a wisp of smoke escape when the casket was moved. My co-worker laughed and said rough weekend. So I thought I had imagined it, a trick of the light, fatigue.

Back after mass to collect the casket, the scene in front of the church: smoke, commotion, buckets of water thrown on a smoking casket, a veritable comedy. And the panicked widow insisting we call the gravediggers immediately, bury him to snuff out the flames. Her husband was afraid of fire.

Some caskets have neon lights to illuminate the body during the viewing, bad luck when unplugging them, a short circuit.

Ꮬ A young woman lying in the grass.

A prosaic bit of tanning, then recurring migraine headaches, hospitalization, death, head opened at autopsy and discovery of a brain eaten away by ants, ants that had lived in her head. Dying of ants in your head.

I will ask how long that takes, decomposition through infestation and, most importantly, is that really possible?

He looks unflappable, so I leave it without asking for more. Sometimes I ask nothing more. Despite my surprise.

He is long past surprise. So I ask few questions.

These lives a long way from me, I am not the embalmer and, even if I were, I wouldn't know any more. Leave room for a little peace and air.

❧ It's a dry wig.

A wig of thick, coarse salt-and-pepper hair, an old woman's wig glued to her head one day with Crazy Glue, glued so it will move no more.

We tried to remove it by tugging a little, no, we had to cut the skin.

At the top of the head is revealed putrefied scalp crawling with wiggling white worms.

❦ The subway.

There were so many over the years at the morgue, I don't even know if we should talk about it, it may be a little dull.

Most don't die. They are disabled for life.

Two causes of death: impact or, more uncommonly, electrocution. Jumping from the platform onto the rails. But no one talks about it much. They were often disfigured. They didn't always have time to hit the ground.

People still don't talk about it, they say not to talk about it so as not to give anyone ideas, give them that little something they were missing to do it themselves. That's what people say.

&. A body that is underwater for a long time.

Swells, the tissue soaks up water, the body triples in size – he mimes the dimensions of the hands of the ten-, twelve-year-old drowning victim, whose body ended up resurfacing after spending some time in a lock.

He picks up the bloated body at the morgue, they ask him to let them know how it goes, he doesn't understand. It's just a drowning victim.

When he sees the inside of the body he understands. The body has no organs. Smooth, smooth, the abdomen has been hollowed out.

An eel enters through the mouth and exits through the opposing orifice and, between the two, eats.

Omnivorous, the *Anguilla rostrata*, the American eel.

❧ Another drowning victim.

Another boy. The corpse starts its descent from one body of water to another, and at the end all that is left are the pelvic bones, a bit of the spine – he gestures the length, not long, a half-metre.

The bones were soft. Soft and polished.

In such cases everything is sealed in a bag, and the bag is put in a casket. That's it.

He recalls: the parents had left clothes. I remember I placed the boy's little clothes in the casket.

❧ He often uses these expressions.

Commonplace. Talking about the morgue, the hospital, they 'release the bodies.'

As if they had been held captive, were under surveillance. Then again, some of them are.

When the bodies are embalmed and ready for the funeral, they 'bring out the bodies.'

A second liberation. They are ready to go.

❧ Another drowning victim.

A child skated on thin ice, stayed underwater from the beginning of the winter until the spring. Ice melting, body resurfacing.

The mother is in the lab, asks for the skates. They are still on his feet, the request is disturbing, then he tells himself she has some ten children, after all.

He unlaces the first skate and pulls gently, but the foot comes off.

In the skate a foot – the mother doesn't want it anymore, she lets it go.

꤮ The beginning of the 1980s.

On the embalming table, a veterinarian who practiced for a few years in Africa. The death certificate says gonorrhea, syphilis, AIDS.

He says all dressed.

He calls my mother to say he will be late. But for once he doesn't touch anything and comes home.

I don't ask more, not whether his colleague took over, nor what the details of this story he is telling me point to or signify. I tell myself, another era, don't want to know.

Adds: AIDS was brand new, I was told I was the one with the most experience. My experience told me not to touch anything.

In the end, I made him up nicely and put him in a box. That's all you're getting.

It was Christmas Eve.

❧ I ask him about AIDS.

He looks for numbers. 1984, three, four cases. 1985, maybe triple that number. 1986, people stop counting.

I ask him about the protocol: there wasn't any, not really, a mandatory declaration on the death certificate, that's it.

Then he thinks: we added nine parts water for one part bleach. We worked in pairs, we passed instruments gloved hand to gloved hand. He talks about it now with a certain levity.

꜅ Six bodies found in the river.

In sleeping bags filled with cement blocks. He will do three of the six. Their faces don't look like faces, rotten flesh, the boxes will be closed, nothing to do but close the boxes.

&. A notorious criminal on the run.

After his most recent serious crime, a bar set on fire, some ten dead, there will be a manhunt. Adds that the criminal hid out for a while near the funeral parlour.

Law enforcement responded, and there were reports that he was shot to death, reports of twenty-nine bullets. Twenty-nine holes.

I didn't do that body. But I saw it at the morgue, I was there for someone else when I found his refrigerated drawer and opened it. You wouldn't be able to do that today.

Rings were drawn around holes in the skin.

But there were at least three times as many. Three times more holes in the skin to take him down. Enforcement indeed.

❧ The body had its throat slit.

The dispatcher at the morgue said a little cut, the man hadn't looked at the body. Everyone knew he was afraid of the dead.

A cross-dresser found in a hotel, a bottle broken, a throat opened, a throat barely holding, an almost severed head.

Being fooled, fooling oneself, when slitting unmasks, when being unmasked is the end. I had to put a turtle-neck on the body.

Did he have to sew, staple? I didn't ask him at the time. Did he have to make it hold, I would ask? No it wasn't staples, but invisible stitches inside to avoid leakage.

Very important.

꩜ He had to cut the bone between the eyes.

In the middle of the brow bone, one centimetre by one centimetre. The rest of the body was to be cremated. That was essential.

Just that bone was of value, frozen with liquid nitrogen, kept in a sterile jar. One day it would be used to clone the man. The request was made twice, the second time he was irritated by the 'disciple' who was required to observe the procedure.

No autopsy had been done. He had to cut the scalp to find the spot, had to saw the skull with a half-moon saw that pivots left to right. The more I cut, the whiter the disciple got. I knew my saw. I gave it a little extra, too close to the brain, and I managed to splatter him, a nice red trail I recall, with a bit of brain.

Tells me afterward, I thought about it, I should have refused, called the police, it was mutilation, that's what it was.

❧ At the diner.

Where we eat and talk about death, there are antiques. I chose this place and out of a sense of ritual decided that all our meetings would take place here.

We realize that it used to be an antique store. Some of the objects that fill the space are guardians of its past – behind me is an old lamp. He will notice it only on the second visit.

A lamp with a metal base that was placed at the exit of the funeral parlour, with dozens of superimposed rings to hold sympathy cards.

❧ In an urn.

Ashes are mainly made up of bone, the rest goes up in smoke.

The smoke can be toxic, lead, mercury, polish, varnish, bodies saturated with drugs, chemicals, embalming products, at least that's the way it was.

Two bodies burnt at the same time, that happened, no matter what they say. Their ashes combined and put in a single urn.

During cremation, some bones stay in the cylinder, and three or four spinning balls crush them into fine ash. Like in a mine with ore, he says, magnets collect screws, plates, because not everything melts, the heat is not intense enough.

An urn contains around 90 percent of the body. The rest is put in a large barrel with other people's remaining 10 percent, and when the barrel is full you empty it.

I read that for the past ten years the deceased's loved ones have been offered a way to turn their ashes into diamonds.

When a baby is cremated, there are no ashes. There is nothing left.

.

Two employees go pick up someone who jumped from a bridge.

Rob him of the thousands of dollars he had on him and falsify documents listing his effects. This would have been simple if the family hadn't known about the money, if the police statement hadn't noted it as well.

They are apprehended at the funeral parlour, they are handcuffed, taken away.

⚚ A veteran.

He was crushed, thought he was a superhero and wanted to stop a high-speed train. It didn't stop.

He says: I would have put him in a small paper bag.

❧ Dogs.

Some funeral homes collected organic waste from hospitals for incineration – there were few crematorium ovens at the time. One night, he accompanied a colleague to avoid staying with the twenty-five cadavers in the lab when there were no embalmings scheduled.

Remembers unloading waste from the dark fridge, dim lighting, bags passed hand to hand, his colleague tripping over a body. A large black dog, a Labrador.

He doesn't add this but I do: a black lab, identical to the one he had years before. That we had. That he loved and had to give up. My sister and I were told it had grown too protective.

Dogs and pigs are the favourite animals for certain experiments in university hospitals. There were scandals in the 1980s. Dog pounds sold dogs to labs at a discount.

They say some still had their collars around their necks.

ᴥ Necrophiliac funeral home employees.

Clearly he saved this for last, put it off – uncomfortable with the stories, he tells me two.

Men raped two dead women.

One in an alley at night, they were bringing her back, she was still in the hearse – she had just hanged herself, the body wasn't even cold.

The other one pulled from the morgue refrigerator – the man was caught in the act by her father who had come to see her for the last time.

❧ A hanging with a zip tie.

And a knife in his pocket because he wasn't sure he wanted to die.

He wanted to be one breath away from death to decide whether he wanted it – he had to see whether it was the right thing to do or if the desire to breathe returned at the brink.

He hadn't realized that with no breath the plan goes awry, that gestures are not precise, that in cutting the plastic tie he would sever his jugular – it wasn't the plan to bleed out like that.

Turns out he wanted to breathe.

⊰ A fireman fails an exam.

Which would have seen him promoted from lieutenant to captain, so he goes home and takes a 22-gauge rifle, kills his wife and two children, then kills himself with a 12-gauge rifle.

The details of models of rifles, he remembers that, but why two different ones, why bother changing guns. The noise and the ammunition the man had on hand, maybe.

The bodies arrive together. He is asked which one he wants to start with. He is the most senior so they let him decide: none, start with none. Go home, go see his wife, his two children. A second refusal to embalm.

He says, you don't forget, he says I often manage to forget, I don't go there.

He says nothing, but I hear it, everything is still there, intact, nothing has moved, how could it?

❧ I have to add that he says everything very quickly, it gets faster every time.

Now the cases are four or five short sentences, and he moves straight on to the next. I don't slow him down but I have time to jot down only a few words, which I manage to reproduce here, most of the time anyway, and they proliferate.

He moves quickly though the short list in front of him, handwritten, folded, unfolded, refolded, folded, refolded, higgledy-piggledy.

Dozens of cases simply titled: The Fireman, The Priest … which he crosses out as he tells them, yellow strokes, a few words that create a sketch and one more yellow stroke. The interviews go fast, are short, a few breakfasts, a few calls.

I don't want to drag it all out of him, drag him out, it's not that – if things appear in flashes then flashes they be.

He goes even faster halfway through the meetings, maybe to get it over with, like the bodies that kept piling up on the lab counter at the end.

He had to go faster.

❧ Conversation with my mother. Unexpected.

I tell her what I am doing with my father. Haven't been together for a long time, but they were when he was practicing. First, surprise, then she remembers. She who normally has a shaky memory, I thought, she starts telling stories in fragments.

As a young man he also went to get bodies by ambulance for the funeral parlour, on top of embalming them. By dint of redoing faces with candle wax he grew skilled, you know, it was an art, he had to make do, be creative, then with the right materials, he achieved excellence, was at the height of his craft, had a reputation, so the most difficult bodies piled up, the cases that weighed the heaviest.

Yes, heavy, he said that, in other words.

She remembers a confused call one afternoon. He was to embalm a little girl with blond hair, at the mother's request put in the casket with the new roller skates she got for her birthday – he called my mother, are the girls there. She didn't understand or at least she didn't truly understand what he was saying.

But I understood well enough.

She also remembers specific details like bodies with gaseous tissue.

They were hard to spot – your father could smell them, they had an indefinable odour, he knew it, they always called him to figure out these things, but he couldn't describe the smell, you had to be there to smell it, that's all.

My father would explain to me, gas accumulates in the body, the tissue, muscles, cartilage, and so on. The body can swell and, when there is too much, it escapes. The smell is horrible. The first time I saw it was in an autopsied body: there were bubbles, it started to boil, bubbles formed in the epidermis. I pierced the skin with a needle. With time, I found the perfect formula, heavy on the formaldehyde. You have to use the right amount. Inject it in the tissue, eradicate the bacteria, the decomposition, as fast as you can. Only once I couldn't detect the presence of gas, it came out after the embalming.

My mother ends by telling me about the nun who had nice black leather slippers, they were too new, much too nice to be buried – some people have strange requests, she laughs, I wanted to keep them for myself, she laughs.

❧ And me.

I have just two memories. I remember my father driving me to a friend's birthday party, in a sort of hearse limo. I was five or six years old and slithering over the seats. When I got there the children greeted me on the balcony with expressions that I didn't recognize immediately. That I would recognize only much later.

And I remember a picture of him in one of our family photo albums. He is wearing a suit, lying in a casket with his hands folded and his eyes closed.

He loves that picture.

✦ A man walks in on his wife with another man.

Doesn't get over it, shoots himself in the head. The woman goes to see her husband in the lab one last time to kiss him.

The eye, which has popped out of its socket, is resting on the cheek. He tells me there is nowhere to kiss him, nothing recognizable as a face or part of one – the chin is still there, maybe, it's the only thing left.

On the chin is where she will kiss her husband for the last time.

❦ A little blond girl, seven or eight years old.

Is it the same one my mother told me about? A winter school trip, her in the front of the toboggan, her friends behind her – you know, the wooden ones that curve up in the front. She jams her feet in there, they start down the hill, the toboggan veers off in the wrong direction, goes straight into a tree, her friends jump, her friends have time, but her feet were too jammed in, her feet stayed in there, her feet got stuck.

It is snowing heavily outside the diner when he tells me about it.

❧ A woman hits a moose.

On Highway 40, she had fur everywhere, the moose was
all over her, she was covered in it, his fur, he says she
looked like a bear. Remove little hair after little hair
after little hair.

ᔌ The harvest.

One day as the harvest was going well, a man disappeared on his own farm – they couldn't figure it out.

Grain is stored in a silo, tons stored that day, things going well that day, then the farmer is found in his silo, a farmer smothered by his seeds, his beautiful bountiful seeds. Grain everywhere, nose, mouth, ears.

I think about the moose fur, and of the two that is the death I prefer – I think of the lack of air and I think of the children hiding in the fridge and the time that goes by as they run out of air.

≈ That's the way it is, I imagine, non-stop for him every day, the incoming, the cases, the dead, the new, and the familiar.

It's like that every day: compare, judge, hesitate, blond children who look alike, then inevitably the categories, hanging, subway, cancer, bullet to the head. Even I ended up lumping the drowning victims together.

There are obviously more anonymous deaths with nothing that stands out – they aren't included here, here are the ones that stand out, we talk mainly about the ones that stand out.

Which perhaps gradually afflicts, when they are all there piled on the lab counter, everywhere, and when you have to lift their heads out of the way to reach the sink. When one makes another appear. Or when they form a line, in your head.

It weighs the weight of all the dead.

❧ I note each case in a few sentences.

In a black notebook, hastily – I don't want to write too much, I don't want to ask for too many details, I follow the rhythm.

Then I go back over each case and mark an X in the margin of the little black notebook that is too small. When it's over, when I have them written down here, I mark an X, and each time I feel lighter, not because something like memory is being rebuilt – it doesn't really have anything to do with me – but because there is one fewer maybe, a question of weight and of what is erected despite the subtraction.

I add and he subtracts, I add and he subtracts, one fewer to write, for me it's simple.

🙢 Two young girls found near a forest.

I ask their age, fourteen or fifteen, killed, raped, ciga-
rette burns all over the bodies, tells me lips, breasts,
buttocks, between the legs.

I don't ask anything else, he is the one who adds: a hair-
brush in the throat.

❧ Yet another body with just a single bone left.

Incinerated head to toe, if you will. A bit of fun during the holidays, a big party, a tall Christmas tree, pretending to light it on fire several times, as a joke.

It's not the first time that something starts as a joke.

And everything goes up in flames, just a few seconds, the building is wood, the people get out as best they can, but it goes fast, as fast as the dozens of people who don't have time to get out. The tragedy leaves some thirty children orphaned.

I didn't know that it was also true what they say, about fire and Christmas trees, particularly when the trees are very dry at the end of December, that they can go up in flames. And the person who pretended to set the Christmas tree on fire, was he the bone?

No, he survived.

❧ During the last interview.

Eventually he says there are no more cases, that we have come to the end of it, as if for a hardship, an ordeal, but he says I will think some more, see what I come up with.

❧ He will get back to me one last time with his memories, this time with funny stories, as he calls them.

Scaring his sister by hanging a funeral wreath on her front door to greet her when she gets home.

Hiding in caskets to terrorize a colleague who is afraid of the dead.

Dressing up in a late bishop's clothes and standing in the shadows to scare an employee working with him at night.

Falling in a grave because the deceased's wife wanted the wreath from the casket, ending up under the casket.

But my mind was already somewhere else.

❧ At the end of our meetings, my father says doctors have found a tumour thirteen millimetres by fifteen millimetres near his left eyeball, which explains why he doesn't see as well on that side, why he suffers from deafness mainly in the left ear.

The tumour was found but not identified, he would have to wait six months to see if it grew – if there is no change it would stay there and that would be that. He would carry on with the thing that isn't changing, and every six months he would have to go back and verify its inactivity.

I don't ask whether I can write it down.

No one says the word *cancer*, not even him, but I think, I can't help it, of his father who died of brain cancer. He told me that the next-door neighbour also died of brain cancer, it's a rare form of cancer, so we tell ourselves there is something else, something to figure out – a friend tells me about basements and radon.

I'm the one who gets carried away, but I go on. Cases of brain tumours are more common among anatomists, pathologists, and embalmers. They think it's the formaldehyde – people point to the greater risk, a highly toxic substance. He is not the one to talk about it so I'm the one who gets carried away. Formaldehyde is an irritating, corrosive, colourless gas. I note that toxicity is everywhere, I find it in my cursory searches and I find it in case histories, it was there every day – understand that this makes me think of all the people who have been handling toxic substances every day for years without knowing it. I write in a notebook what I have to avoid swallowing, touching, having, breathing: polyvinyl chloride, diethylhexyl phthalate, or diisononyl bisphenol A, oxybenzone parabens of shower curtains, cleansers, cosmetics, tin cans, sunscreens, Teflon, nail polish, toothpaste.

❧ After years of embalming, walks away.

Suddenly. He and my mother had separated shortly beforehand.

He would work as a painter, seam caulker, heavy machinery operator, a few years in a mine in northern Quebec, from small to large, big, heavy, scrap metal, residue, metals, one-and-a-half kilometres underground.

What is removed from the ground and brought to the surface.

Was it a transition to a more permanent world, even though it never really is, less laden but more disembodied? Perhaps it's not that simple. Still being near what is underground. But the bodies – dead, disintegrated, desecrated, betrayed, struck down – are not so deep underground. There is copper and zinc. Maybe a bit of gold.

The last morning we met, he told me about a monstrous machine, the largest there is, told me about the power of the engines, the size of the wheels. Crawler, crane, shovel, spreader, excavator.

I ask him about what I call walking away.

The shift from fascination to revulsion, I hear, out of steam, another world, negative and, above all, I wanted to leave peacefully in the morning like everyone with my lunch box.

❧ As this comes to a close, draws to an end.

My father is called for the job he has been dreaming about for years, four thousand kilometres away. This time in an open-pit mine.

Epilogue

❦ My father left that dream job and time went by.

My father's tumour didn't grow.

But in the meantime, while we were waiting to see whether it would grow, a tumour was found in my mother's colon, the size of a grapefruit, they said.

An emergency operation, intensive care, and her disease.

Chemotherapy, then the glimpse of a recovery, short-lived. A relapse, more chemotherapy, then intensive care and palliative care and spending time together and watching over her and eventually waiting for her death. And saying goodbye.

My mother's death at age fifty-nine, just like that, while I was more worried for my father.

She asked him one morning, as a sort of reconciliation, to handle her funeral arrangements, which he did.

I'll come back to that, I will have to come back to that, see what I come up with.